KILLING TIME IN KENTON

Killing Time in Kenton

A WINIFRED SMY MYSTERY

Michael Heath

Fara Press

This edition published in 2022 by Fara Press, Stowmarket IP14 6JH.

Cover design by Lucy Johnson

ISBN details:
978-1-7390982-0-9 (Print version)
978-1-7390982-1-6 (eBook)

First Edition

1

A Folly is Set in Train

If England were an unmade bed, then its most rumpled sheets would be at the centre, running vertically up from the Peak District, through the dales of Yorkshire and the Northern Pennines, before spreading out in the great county of Northumberland. On the right-hand side of the bed would be the gentle, almost smooth, folds that are East Anglia, where the hills are low, and the landscape cowers beneath vast skies.

Suffolk sits between worldly Essex and remote Norfolk and is quite unlike either. A county so unambitious that it has no city and even the names of its rivers remain unknown to all but Suffolkers. But what names those beautiful rivers bear: the Blyth, the Waveney, the Stour, and the Alde.

Follow the River Deben inland from its tidal estuary and you pass the beautiful market town of Woodbridge. Continuing west from Woodbridge, the Deben's diminishing and uncertain watery path skirts small villages with ancient churches, laps against banks lined with reedmace, loosestrife, and willow, and murmurs contentedly under sleepy stone bridges. It leads us into the hidden byways and people of East Suffolk where the dialect carries the low purr of a cat and the hours and minutes of a bee-loud summer day seem to falter and stall.

Lying at the heart of this unassuming region sits the village of Debenham. Its main street is fringed with shops and houses – from the Mediaeval to the late Victorian – that stand shoulder to shoulder like a hastily attired rag-tag rebel army.

Follow the slope of the main street to the bottom and you encounter the Deben again. In the summer, its bed is parched and it sleeps like a drunk in the hot sun. But when the rains of winter gather in East Suffolk and the clouds move low and heavy over the landscape, then the Deben is an animal, growling and gushing until it rises above its banks and rolls out and over on to the streets, wilfully washing into the homes that lie perilously adjacent to it.

So it was with a sense of quiet astonishment that the people of this unremarkable area learned of the building of a new railway. A venture endorsed by self-important men convinced of the prosperity it would introduce to these time-worn villages. It would connect farm to city and port, carrying cattle and produce to all the markets of the country and even beyond. The line would penetrate to the agricultural heart of the county bringing pounds, population and progress. Before the railway, East Suffolk was a forgotten tract of the country waiting to be liberated by the all-conquering genius of industry and finance; and now, with every railway sleeper that was laid, came the inching tide of modernity that would herald a new dawn for this disregarded corner. The Mid Suffolk Light Railway – or 'The Middy' as it came to be known by local people - was a new beginning, a new tomorrow.

Until the money ran out.

Instead of finding itself connected by a web of radiating strands to the other lines that bisected the county, the railway became a melancholy, amputated road to nowhere. Leaving the main junction at Haughley, the spur sallied bravely across the fields only to peter out in open pastures by the village of Cratfield. There was a roll-call of small settlements that it ran towards but never quite within: Mendlesham, Brockford and Wetheringsett, Aspall and Thorndon, Kenton, Worlingworth, Horham, Stradbroke, Wilby and Laxfield.

Despite bankruptcies, resignations, pitiful under-investment and public disinterest, it lurched on. Train drivers and their firemen were instructed to open the level crossing gates themselves in an effort to cut costs. And though the farmers occasionally used the service, the gradual arrival of the motor vehicle soon began to hammer the nails – one by one – into the coffin lid of the doomed enterprise.

Almost at the centre of the line sat Kenton Junction, situated a mile from the village from which it took its name. The station and the village seemed resentfully huddled in their respective quarters like two lovers refusing to make up after an argument. But the 'Junction' that had been added so ostentatiously to the name was a verbal folly, in the same way that the whole line was a folly of men's complacency and greed. The spur line that was supposed to break from the main line and link up with the outskirts of Ipswich via Debenham was never completed. Again, as the money to pay the contractors dwindled away, so the track ignominiously ended a mile from Debenham village, and silently died there.

The single utilitarian building that sat on Kenton Junction's concrete platform housed a booking office at one end and a store for goods and parcels at the other. Between was an open area capped by a small canopy, inside which the few passengers that used the line could wait.

Very little occurred of any interest in Kenton - either in the village, its station or the surrounding fields and shallow valleys - until one gusty mid-morning on the 5th of April, 1910. Whilst the Red Poll cattle ambled over the nearby field and wing-flicking dunnocks scampered along the damp turf of the roadside, the devil himself was hovering above the parish.

2

A Sleeping Furrener

At first glance, Percy Whiting, Station Master at Kenton, thought that the man slumped in the corner of the small waiting shelter was asleep. The railway official cleared his throat and was about to gently tap him on the shoulder to awaken him but, when he saw how finely dressed the sleeping man was, decided against it.

Instead, in a kindly voice he asked, "Excuse me, sir."

But the man didn't reply.

Whiting bent down low and peered up at the resting man's face, which had been hidden by a hat that was inelegantly tilted forward. To Whiting's horror, he realised that the man wasn't sleeping: he was dead. His glassy, lifeless eyes staring down at the station shelter floor.

Shocked by the man's ghastly expression, the Station Master stepped slowly backwards out of the canopied shelter. He desperately looked around for someone who might help but the station was now deserted, with the two railway porters busy in the engine shed. Tuesday's 10.23 am train to Laxfield - still within earshot as it pulled its heavy carriages towards Worlingworth - had just departed.

Whiting panicked and ran towards the engine shed, shouting the names of his two porters. The tramp of their heavy boots could soon be heard as they and the panting figure of the Station Master ran back towards the station platform. They then walked slowly to the station shelter, but no one was now prepared to enter. Slowly, respectfully, each man reached up and removed his hat.

Later that afternoon, when Superintendent Freeman and his Inspector, Herbert Tranmer, had arrived on the scene from Framlingham police station, it was to find Debenham's own policeman, George Cornish, guarding the body that was still occupying the corner of the waiting room. A man often given to feelings of self-importance, Cornish was relishing the moment and, having dispatched the two porters and station master to a respectful distance, interposed himself between the waiting room and the small audience of villagers who had now gathered on the opposite platform.

The Superintendent, a man that always appeared to carry the worries of the entire world on his rounded shoulders, glanced rather cursorily at the pompous guard of honour.

"Good afternoon. It's Cornish, isn't it?"

Superintendent Freeman removed his glasses and wiped them on the lining of his coat.

"Good afternoon, Sir. We're 'onoured that you should come as well, Sir."

"I was informed that the deceased was a man of, shall we say, the 'better classes', Cornish, so thought it prudent to attend. Have you inspected the body?"

"Yes, Sir. Sudden death, I reckon. I fare an 'eart attack."

Inspector Tranmer, in a broad Yorkshire accent that curiously jarred with Cornish's soft Suffolk brogue, interjected. "Did you know the man at all?"

"No, Sir. A furrener we think. Hal a bit from these parts."

"Sorry, Constable?"

The Superintendent put his glasses back on and wearily explained, "He means certainly not from round here. Suffolk dialect, Tranmer. You'll soon pick it up."

"Oh, of course, Sir."

"Let's see the body, Cornish."

Freeman and Tranmer entered the waiting room and crouched down to take a closer look.

"Has anyone moved the body, Cornish?" Superintendent Freeman called back.

"Don't think so, Sir. I cycled straight here from Deb'nham and only Station Master Whiting and the two porter lads were here a'riddy."

The stiff brightness of the April sun had made the heavily shadowed interior of the waiting shelter all the darker, but Tranmer still noticed that blood had trickled through the fingers of the man's right hand that was placed upon his chest. He carefully teased apart each side of the expensive greatcoat, revealing a dark bloody plume which had spread across the lower abdomen.

"Something not right here, Sir," he whispered.

Superintendent Freeman reached forward and lifted the dead man's right hand. What they saw caused both men to audibly gasp, which soon brought Cornish into the waiting room to see what had happened.

"Find something, Sir?"

"Oh yes, Cornish, we've found something. This man hasn't had a heart attack. I would say that this man has been murdered."

Cornish was temporarily dazed by the news and could think of nothing more to ask than, "Are you sure?"

"Quite sure. And the murder weapon is still buried in the poor blighter's chest. Have a look for yourself."

Cornish absent-mindedly removed his helmet and looked sideways at the corpse, thinking that somehow it would soften the terrible sight. He'd seen death many times, but this was the first occasion in his 12 years in the force that he had looked upon a murder victim.

The Inspector peered closely to see what it was that had been lying under the bloodied hand that had tried, instinctively and in vain, to remove the weapon.

"What is that, Tranmer? It's like a large corkscrew."

"It's not a corkscrew, Superintendent, it's a screw gimlet."

It was the voice of a woman, and the three men jerked their heads around as one to see who had the impertinence to interrupt their criminal inspection.

"And you are?"

The woman, tall and straight, with a stare that would not back down under the interrogative gazes of the three policemen, stood confidently just outside the station shelter. Her pale complexion was lined with the first shallow etching of middle age, and the loose sleeves of her light blue blouse were fanned by a bluster of breezes that scurried along the open track.

"My name, as you so politely asked, is Winifred Smy. Oh, Good Morning, Constable Cornish."

"Well, Mrs Smy..."

"*Miss* Smy," she defiantly replied.

The Superintendent started again. "Well, Miss Smy, do I need to remind you that this is a police matter and not the place for... for a woman?"

"A reminder is not appropriate as no one has yet brought that obvious fact to my attention. And, putting aside the patronising remark about my gender, I proffered some information that might be useful in your investigations. But, as I can see that you three *very* superior and *very* intelligent men have no need of anything a mere woman could contribute, I will – with your official approval, of course – continue with my errands."

Winifred Smy gave the smallest nod of her head which, coupled with the penetrating gaze that accompanied it, conveyed a steely mockery of authority that all three policemen instantly felt. She moved slowly and on her own terms, glancing once more at the slumped corpse as if to show that such sights were both familiar and held no horror for her.

Freeman watched her as she walked away before saying in a low voice to Tranmer, "What a damned impudent woman."

Cornish smiled knowingly, brushing the metal badge on his helmet with his sleeve before carefully putting it back on.

Once the body had been further inspected, it was covered and removed to the back of a waiting horse-drawn farmer's cart, which then made its way sluggishly along the Eye Road with a small retinue of children in attendance.

Superintendent Freeman suggested to Tranmer that he return to Framlingham and gather some personal effects before finding lodgings that evening back in Kenton. There would have to be extensive enquiries; no one even knew who the murdered man was, never mind who his killer might be.

Hearing this, Cornish suggested to Inspector Tranmer that 'The Crown' public house, at the junction of the Eye and Debenham roads, would always give him a room. Consequently, the following day found Tranmer organising his few clothes in one of the pub's small bedrooms, which were usually occupied by the itinerant agents of various agricultural suppliers.

News of Tuesday's murder in Kenton had rapidly spread amongst the neighbouring parishes, and all conversation either began with the lurid details of the murder or inevitably gravitated towards it. In the village of Kenton itself, long-acquainted neighbours now cautiously eyed each other as suspicion and rumour insidiously settled amongst them.

On the morning of Thursday 7th April, two days after the murder, Inspector Tranmer left The Crown and set out along the Eye Road towards Kenton station. On the previous day, enquiries made in the surrounding villages and farmhouses meant that matters were now moving quickly, and he strode with the breezy confidence of a man whose destiny was certain. Just as he was passing a cottage that stood on the adjacent corner to the village church, there emerged the purposeful figure of Winifred Smy carrying several books.

"Morning, *Miss* Smy." He raised his hat, whilst deliberately emphasising the word 'Miss' in a provocative allusion to their first meeting.

But the provocation went unheeded.

"Inspector? Good morning. Have you got your murderer yet?"

"We very soon will have. I admit you were right about the murder weapon. It was indeed a screw gimlet and, what's more, we now know who the murderer is."

"Have you arrested him?"

"I am meeting PC Cornish and a colleague from Thorndon in 15 minutes' time to do that very thing."

"So, you think it was a Kenton man, do you?"

"I certainly do."

"Well, then you must arrest him. But can I tell you something?" Winifred Smy looked coolly up into the inspector's face. "I am quite convinced that you are about to arrest the wrong man."

3

Suspect the Certain

"Your opinion is of little interest to me, Miss Smy. This is a police matter, and we don't welcome the contribution of any budding amateur detectives."

Tranmer wiped the brim of his hat and carefully put it back on. Despite his brusque response, Miss Smy could see that his face was kindly and wondered if he had developed his detached and rather austere manner to protect the tender and emotional character that lay beneath. His almost black hair was now greying at the temples and the angle of Tranmer's dark-blue eyes seemed to betray some undefined inner sadness.

"Surely the phrase 'budding amateur' is a tautology, Inspector? But I do believe I have the right to an opinion on a grave event that has taken place in our village, detective or not. Or perhaps you are of the mind that we in Kenton are not entitled to our opinions?"

"Of course, you have the right to your opinions, but that doesn't mean, with the greatest respect, Miss Smy, that they are *informed* opinions."

Winifred Smy eyed the Inspector closely, rather enjoying seeing Tranmer's overweening pride rattled. She knew the stern carapace was cracking.

"Whereas your opinion, unlike ours, is very much *informed.* I believe that is what you are saying?"

Tranmer vaguely nodded, irritated that the serenity that he had felt only minutes before as he'd walked down the Eye Road had now utterly vanished.

Miss Smy held up the spines of the books she was carrying to view them. Without looking up, she added, "Then you must pursue your informed opinion, even if it means that you are about to arrest a man for a crime that was not of his doing."

"Miss Smy, I have - as of yesterday - become aware of facts that will clearly show that the balance of probabilities..."

"But a murder trial will not be interested in your 'balance of probabilities'. I'm sure you're aware of that? A case such as this will stand or fall on it being 'beyond reasonable doubt'. Isn't that what a criminal court will require?"

"Yes, of course," Tranmer reluctantly conceded.

"And if a mere budding amateur, such as I, can raise questions that cannot yet be answered, what would a skilled defence lawyer make of your prosecution evidence, Inspector?"

Tranmer's lips pursed with the ignominy of having allowed this conversation to continue, and he stepped away with the intention of accommodating the impertinence of Miss Smy no longer.

"I can see you need to leave, Inspector. I know I am rather annoying in my conversation, but would you allow me a final personal question before you do?"

"If you must," the Inspector sighed.

"What brought you to Suffolk? Perhaps you have suffered a recent loss?"

"Miss Smy, you really are..."

"Am I right?"

"Well, actually..." the remaining words were soon lost in Tranmer's throat.

"I thought so. I'm sorry, it was rather an impertinent thing to ask. I do hope that it wasn't your wife?"

Tranmer could only stare with complete incredulity at this strange woman that fate had hurled into his life. Yet gradually, his features softened before he reached into an inside jacket pocket. From his wallet, he took a small photograph, looked fondly at it for a moment and then handed it to her.

Miss Smy inspected the photograph and returned it to him.

"I'm very sorry, Inspector. A very lovely woman."

"How did you know?"

"Oh, just a wild guess. Little things, I suppose. I noticed that your shirt has not been ironed where you believe it would not show. Where it does show, one perceives that you iron with the skill of, dare I say, a 'budding amateur'. You wear a wedding ring but, when I overheard Cornish suggest you stay at The Crown, you immediately assented which suggested that you had no loved one with whom to confer about any sudden temporary change of address."

"That's very astute of you," said Tranmer, self-consciously smoothing his shirt against his chest.

"You are a Yorkshireman, a bustling county where you had, I am sure, many opportunities to further your profession. And yet here you are in a rural, underpopulated county where only the retirement of a superior will afford you any career progression."

"So, you think I am running away?"

"No, Inspector. Not running away but running towards. Towards peace of mind, perhaps. To be rid of every reminder, every signpost that points to a happier time that is now lost."

Winifred Smy's sentence faltered a little and she appeared to become momentarily preoccupied, yet soon gathered her momentum again to ask, "But that is not the chief reason I wanted to ask my personal question of you."

"I'm not sure I want to hear what your 'chief reason' is, Miss Smy. But I'm sure I am going to."

"Thank you, Inspector, for now I return to our murder. You have very recently started your employment in Framlingham and are, naturally, eager to show your worth. This is laudable when your profession is a teacher, an apprentice blacksmith or, perhaps, a new bailiff; but eagerness to impress when you are a newly arrived Police Inspector unsettles me somewhat."

"And that's what you believe, is it? That I have suddenly thrown years of experience to one side just so I can show Superintendent Freeman that I know what I am doing?"

"Yes, Inspector, that is exactly what I believe."

Miss Smy exhibited the same defiant stare that she had first shown when they had met only two days previously.

"Miss Smy, one thing I know about being a police officer is that I make no decision until I have assembled the facts."

"But that is exactly my point! I do not doubt that you have doggedly pursued the facts, but you have done so based on a conclusion that you formed two days ago when you were at the train station. You and your fellow officers have expertly gathered those facts that point absolutely to your chief suspect, but not to the real murderer."

"So, perhaps you'd like to tell me what my conclusion was, as you seem to know so much about what I think, Miss Smy?"

Winifred Smy smiled and calmly walked on, compelling the Inspector to follow.

"On Tuesday you discovered that the murder weapon was a screw gimlet. A fearsome enough thing with a dreadful long spike that was pushed into the chest of Mr Carr-Pettiford and instantly killed him."

"So you know who was murdered?"

"Why, of course, Inspector. The whole village knows! But you must let me continue."

Tranmer wearily assented.

"I am sure that, very soon afterwards, you will also have discovered that a screw gimlet is a tool peculiar to the trades of carpenters and wheelwrights. From this, you must therefore have naturally deduced that the only person that could have owned it was Kenton's carpenter, Mr Robert Knights. You had a suspect, Inspector, now all you needed was a motive."

Miss Smy waved vigorously at two farm hands retrieving a fallen hawthorn tree that had toppled into a field ditch, before continuing her hypothesis.

"It is well known in Kenton and beyond that Robert Knights' wife, Arabella, is wracked with tuberculosis; that the income of that household has suffered because she is unable to work, and Knights has struggled to care for her whilst endeavouring to earn his living. Your 'facts' have also revealed that he was seen near the murder scene on Tuesday morning. It is a small step to thus conclude that Knights was presented with an irresistible opportunity to acquire a substantial sum by murdering an obviously wealthy man waiting on Kenton's station platform."

She turned to the Inspector with a searching look. "How am I doing so far, Inspector?" She noticed that Tranmer had loosened his tie whilst she'd been talking.

"These facts thoroughly corroborate your original theory. The conclusion is neat, easily verifiable and, no doubt, will serve notice to the East Suffolk Police that you are a man of great promise. All that remains to do is to meet with Cornish and the good officer from Thorndon village and bring the whole unfortunate incident to a satisfying close. You will search the carpenter's dwelling and workshop and will, no doubt, find some missing item that Mr Carr-Pettiford was carrying before he was brutally slain. This fortuitous discovery will be the final nail of evidence in the coffin of poor Mr Knights."

Tranmer clapped a slow, mocking applause.

"Bravo, Miss Smy! But it doesn't alter the fact that I am now to apprehend the murderer. Facts are facts. It's quite nonsense to think otherwise."

"Inspector Tranmer, that summary I have just given you is exactly what the murderer wants you to think! A snare has been cunningly set and you have unwittingly stepped right into it."

The Inspector could contain his irritation no longer. "I resent that imputation! I resent your wild theories and your deeply disrespectful manner, Miss Smy."

"Perhaps I am disrespectful. But I have learned in life to always suspect the certain and pursue the doubt. Inspector Tranmer, your path leads to the grisly hanging of an innocent Kenton villager."

"And your path, Miss Smy? Where does your path lead, I wonder?"

"Why, to the murderer, of course."

4

Inspector Tranmer Considers a Smoking Jacket

Winifred Smy stood in the garden that opened out behind her Kenton cottage, cradling a cup of warm tea, watching as the morning sun caressed the east-facing wall of the church tower. A small flock of rooks were arguing within the bare black branches of a horse chestnut, their deep, short caws ricocheting above the graves.

It had already been a difficult few hours. Much earlier that morning, after making sure that her mother was comfortable, she had walked to the small house and workshop where the Knights lived. There, she attended to Robert Knights' wife, Arabella, whose weight loss from the final stages of consumption was now so severe that she appeared almost childlike and small in the bed.

"Is that you, Fred?" whispered Arabella, hoarsely. The shortening of Winifred to 'Fred' had begun in school, and she only allowed those she long knew to use this familiarity.

"It's me." Miss Smy sat by the bed and took Arabella's hand in hers. Her temperature was alarmingly high, and the emaciated body jerked with the incessant cough that was slowly killing her. Dabbing a cold compress against the feverish forehead, Miss Smy asked, "Have you slept?"

Arabella Knights closed her eyes and shook her head. "That fool Cornish and his cronies came and took my Robert. Mind yew, at least he won't have to hear me ratticken around when he's tryin' to sleep. But why dew they think he did it? Robert wouldn't hurt a fly, Fred. Yew know it."

"Don't you worry, Bella, he'll be home soon, and he will look after you. I promise."

"Will he? Old Mary says the same, but I know she don't half talk a load a' squit."

Miss Smy smiled reassuringly but thought of how white Arabella now looked. What was the Keats line she recalled? *"Youth grows pale, and spectre thin, and dies."* Yes, Keats himself had witnessed the cruel, final stages of consumption.

It was a loud knock at her front door that startled Winifred Smy out of her thoughts and back into the cold sunshine of her own garden. She opened the door to find a serious-looking Inspector Herbert Tranmer with his hat already removed.

"Good morning, Miss Smy. I was wondering if I might have a few minutes?"

She directed him to the kitchen table and offered tea, which he declined. Tranmer looked a little awkward and, noticing a half-eaten slice of bread and butter, suggested, "Shall I call back? You've not finished your breakfast."

"No, I can't eat it. Food has long since ceased to have any pleasure for me. A passing stay in a London prison saw to that."

Miss Smy could see from Tranmer's confused features that he was unable to follow the line of her allusion, so she asked instead, "I hear you arrested Robert Knights, after all?"

Tranmer was pleased to be back on safer conversational territory. "The focus of our enquiries has yielded up our man. We also found Mr Carr-Pettiford's wallet hidden in the workshop. I am pleased to say we have our murderer."

"The focus of your enquiries has yielded up your chief suspect, not the murderer. And, yesterday, I went so far as to predict that you would find other evidence. You were meant to."

Tranmer couldn't stop himself from betraying a dismissive smirk. He sat back in the chair, causing its joints to release a squeal of pain as they accommodated his weight.

"I have my murderer and you have your theories, Miss Smy. But the reason for my call was to let you know that, having now concluded my investigation, I have vacated my room at The Crown and intend moving back to Framlingham this afternoon."

"I feel honoured that you should want to let me know you're leaving."

"I am certain that you see me as nothing more than a bluff policeman, but I hold you in high regard, Miss Smy, despite our differences. I appreciate that you had a certain view of what happened on Tuesday, but you must remember that not all the evidence that we uncovered was in the public view. Nevertheless, I was rather struck by your observations, I don't mind admitting."

"I feel that you are trying to flatter me, Inspector. You must know I am not the type that takes kindly to flattery."

"Oh, I wouldn't doubt that for a moment. And now, that said, I must be going."

Tranmer looked as if he wanted to add something else, his mouth awkwardly opening a little to begin to speak, yet a certain embarrassment overtook him. Instead, he rose from his chair and walked out of the kitchen to the front door, with Miss Smy following.

"Goodbye, Ma'am. If ever I return to Kenton, then I would be very happy to make your acquaintance again. On non-police matters, of course."

She shook his hand and turned to go back into her cottage. Over her shoulder, she threw back, "Oh, Inspector. How did you explain that jacket?"

"What jacket?"

"Oh, didn't you know? Mr Whiting, the Station Master, said it was a most curious thing."

Tranmer knew this was the moment he should walk away, but such was the teasing cadence of Miss Smy's remark, his commitment, once again, failed him.

"I'm sorry, but I don't quite follow."

"Oh, it was nothing really. Only I asked Mr Whiting – I think it was the day after the murder - whether there had been anything unusual that morning before he had found the body.

At first, he said 'no', there had been nothing out of the ordinary. But then he remembered the strange matter of a burning jacket. Apparently, it caused quite a fuss."

Reluctantly intrigued, Tranmer edged slowly back towards Miss Smy.

"He didn't tell me."

Miss Smy smiled impishly. "Perhaps you didn't ask him?"

He flinched momentarily but said nothing.

"Mr Whiting said that the 10.23 am train stopped on time at Kenton station. He was just chatting with the engine driver – and Mr Bloom the fireman – when someone from a carriage shouted that there was a fire on the other side of the train. Of course, all three men rushed to see what it was and found a burning jacket that must have been hurled out of the train window. Mr Whiting was sure that it had been doused in something. He thought petrol. It took a long time for them to put it out. There are still scorch marks on the paintwork of the carriage, I believe."

"I still don't see the relevance."

"Then you must look for the relevance. Oh, and then there was the rather enlightening conversation I had with Mrs Chevallier."

"Mrs Chevallier from Aspall Hall? Where Carr-Pettiford was staying? I spoke to her myself. She had very little to tell me."

"No, she had very little you wanted to hear. They are very different things, Inspector."

Winifred Smy's attention was taken by the lemony yellow of some primroses huddling under a hedge. "How very beautiful. Are you a gardener, Inspector?"

"No, I'm not."

"Oh, but you should be. It teaches one the value of patience."

"Perhaps you could tell me more about this conversation with Mrs Chevallier? I really do have to get back to Framlingham."

"Dear Mrs Chevallier and I often meet up. We first met in London some years ago. Of course, our intercourse very much revolved around the murder, especially as Mr Carr-Pettiford was staying with the Chevalliers at the time. She said she was bothered by one small detail, which she couldn't for the life of her resolve. All to do with Mr Carr-Pettiford's motor car."

"What about it?"

"Well, the first thing she shared was that Mr Carr-Pettiford detested trains. He has owned one of these new motor cars for two or three years now and, so Mrs Chevallier informed me, would never use anything else when he travelled. On the morning of the murder, he told Mrs Chevallier that he was meeting someone at the station. Of course, as he didn't mention which station, she naturally assumed that it must be the small station at Aspall."

Unpersuaded that this clue had any relevance to the case, Tranmer looked irritatedly at Winifred Smy. "Well, Miss Smy, that's where we found his car. So, he'd obviously parked the car at Aspall and taken the train to Kenton. It's the very next stop. The Station Master at Aspall saw him waiting."

"But that's what I don't understand, Inspector. You see, if I loathed trains and owned a very expensive motor car, and was meeting someone at Kenton, then I would drive there. Aspall Hall is some distance from Aspall station, and there are at least two roads that would have got Mr Carr-Pettiford to Kenton much quicker – and he would have avoided the transport he so detested."

"Miss Smy, I am at a loss as to how all this pertains to the murder."

"Then think very hard, Inspector. It's so obvious. The person he was meeting was at Aspall, not Kenton. Not once did he mention Kenton to Mrs Chevallier. And that very fact wholly exonerates Robert Knights. I grant you that Mr Knights was seen at Kenton Station on the morning of the murder, but he never left the parish all morning. I have witnesses to that. Oh, and one more fact I have learned: I understand from the Station Master at Aspall that Mr Carr-Pettiford never even purchased a ticket."

"This is all nonsense, Miss Smy. Carr-Pettiford somehow forgot to buy a ticket. It's easy enough in a small station which is often unmanned. He was probably going to pay when he got to his destination. For whatever reason, Carr-Pettiford took the train to Kenton, Knights saw an opportunity for some easy money and killed him. It's as plain as day."

"You're wrong, Inspector. Why has the person Mr Carr-Pettiford was supposed to be meeting never made himself known? I believe that you found his appointment diary. Was there an entry for the day of the murder?"

"Oh, it just said 'B' and the time of 10.15 am against it."

"Then that confirms it. The train departs Aspall station at 10.18 precisely. Whoever he met at 10.15 am, must have been waiting at Aspall Station."

"Then how do you account for the fact that his body was discovered at Kenton Station, not Aspall?"

"Oh, that's quite simple. By the time he reached Kenton Station, he was already dead."

5

Walter Bullingham Goes Off the Rails

It was the usual busy Friday market day in Debenham. The lowing of cows, mechanical clucking of hens and anxious whinnying of horses all combined with the shouts and hollers of the villagers, who were disagreeing, berating and greeting one another across the green. Farmers, horsemen, shepherd boys and agricultural labourers formed small conspiratorial groups, trading gossip, farm prices and salty anecdotes of questionable veracity.

The sun that had vainly tried to warm the lengthening days of early April had now ceased to show itself, giving way to grey-tinged clouds which were being hurriedly ushered across the sky by a bullying, chill wind.

Winifred Smy moved slowly through the throng, occasionally smiling at those she knew, and gently nodding to those she was less familiar with. She had, that morning, left a book for her friend, Mrs Chevallier, at Aspall Hall and then walked on from there to Debenham to do a little shopping for that evening's meal.

As she reached the bottom of the High Street, she saw the large, imposing frame of Mrs Bullingham emerge from Abbotts' shop. To Winifred Smy's dismay, Mrs Bullingham had also spotted her, and immediately walked through the crowd towards her.

"Not too cold for you, Miss Smy?"

"Warm enough. I've been walking most of the morning. How are you and Mr Bullingham?"

"Best as can be. But I hear'd you have a new man in your life?"

"Have I? No one told me."

Elizabeth Bullingham always had an intimidating habit of pursing her lips when she was being sarcastic - and being sarcastic was her favoured style of talking with most people.

"Well, a policeman's lady isn't one to blabber, I fare."

"Mrs Cornish doesn't seem to think so. Ask PC Cornish."

Mrs Bullingham suspected that she was going to come off worse in this round of verbal sparring, so changed the subject. "Anyway, I hear'd that they've let that Robert Knights go free. Why would they let a murderer walk free, Miss Smy? What's your new man-friend told you about that?"

"I wouldn't know about any news from a man-friend as I remain as unattached today as I was yesterday, last month and last year. Perhaps you heard it from Mrs Cornish?"

There was the slightest grimace detectable on the puffy features of Mrs Bullingham's face. She was a large woman or, as she was often cruelly described by others in Debenham, 'big-boned'. When suitably roused by drink, she would taunt the men of the village to an arm-wrestling match, but very few accepted and even fewer could best her. And yet she also had a reputation for neatness both in her dress and labour.

"And how is Mr Bullingham? Business is good, I hope?"

"'Int ser likely, as long as that idiot husband of mine is in charge. He wouldn't know a shrewd business move if it punched 'im in his tater trap."

"Well, let's hope that 1910 holds better fortune for Mr Bullingham than 1909."

"He's a'riddy thrown away most of his money as you well know. Madcap railway schemes and the loike. He's barely making enough now to get by. And the day he goes down, me and my little boy go down with him."

Miss Smy found herself wrestling with feelings of compassion for Mrs Bullingham. It was true, she was loathed by most people in the village, and her physical size was openly ridiculed by the village children, but she was tethered to a husband whose business dealings had been reckless. Whatever Miss Smy felt about the character of Mrs Bullingham, she knew that she had suffered at the hands of her husband's poor judgement.

"I think fate was rather unkind in those matters," said Miss Smy with genuine feeling. Mrs Bullingham looked away, openly uncomfortable with anyone's sympathy.

"Well, Mrs Bullingham, I must get back to Kenton. Enjoy the rest of your day."

As Miss Smy was walking past Tollgate Cottage, she saw PC Cornish cycling towards her along the Aspall Road. He had a curious relationship with his bicycle, always riding with his body at a slight angle as if he was very slowly toppling both himself and the machine to the ground. He stopped shakily but rapidly recovered his usual air of arrogance and superiority.

"Lovely to see you, PC Cornish. And how is your wife?"

"Bit of a tizzick these last few days, but good otherwise. I suppose you've a'riddy 'eard the news?"

"That Mr Knights has been released from prison? Yes, I was told yesterday. I am glad the Inspector changed his mind."

Cornish's face grew solemn. "Oh no, Miss Smy. That wasn't what I was going to say. The news I meant was about his wife, Mrs Knights."

"Arabella? Has she...?"

"'Fraid so, Miss Smy. Just cycled back from Kenton. Died barely an 'our ago."

"Oh...and Mr Knights. Was he with her?"

"He was, Ma'am. He's taken it 'ard."

"I was with her only yesterday. It doesn't seem possible."

"It's a terrible thing. Watching 'em just waste away an' all."

Winifred Smy looked away so that Cornish wouldn't see how deeply affected she had been by the news. The fact that she knew such news was imminent did not soften the force of its blow. She and Arabella were almost the same age and had spent several years together in Kenton School. She remembered the games, the fights, the making up and the sharing of what the future might bring for each. Their paths had diverged in very different ways. Arabella remained in Kenton whilst Miss Smy believed that only London might satisfy her youthful pretensions.

She steadied herself whilst Cornish, to his credit, pretended to flick through some pages in his police notebook.

"Thank you for letting me know. I will have to get back and see if there is anything I can do. Oh, PC Cornish, before I go, can I ask you a question?"

"Of course. If I can answer might be another thing."

"Mr Bullingham once lost a lot of money. I never quite understood how. Do you know?"

PC Cornish nodded knowingly and rubbed the back of his neck. "I do know, although he didn't want it to get out."

Then, to Miss Smy's surprise, the expression on the policeman's face quickly changed, as if something had suddenly sprung to mind.

"Cood a hell! That's where I first saw 'im! I knew I knew 'is face. I should 'ave recognised 'im when they'd laid 'im out."

"I'm sorry, PC Cornish. Recognised whom? Mr Bullingham?"

"No, not Mr Bullingham, I don't mean 'im, Miss Smy. Mr Carr-Pettiford! That's who I'm rememberen. Took a while 'cos it's been a good few years since I first saw 'im."

"I'm intrigued. Where did you first meet Mr Carr-Pettiford?"

"In Deb'nham of course. He was with Mr Chevallier and they were talken up the new railway that was to go right through Deb'nham all the way to West'rham, by Ipswidge. Must be ten years ago or so now. Red Lion it was. In the big room. A lot of fancy talken about buying shares in this new light railway and 'ow it would be wonderful and bring lots of trade to the village!"

"PC Cornish, are you saying that Mr Carr-Pettiford had been here before? Selling shares in a railway?"

"Too roight! And what idiot dew yew think bought most of 'em?"

"Walter Bullingham?"

"Walter Bullingham!"

"How interesting, PC Cornish. How very interesting."

6

Inspector Tranmer Rights his Wrongs

As she crouched beside the grave of Arabella Knights, who had only been interred that morning, Winifred Smy thought of the things the deceased had been denied or granted in her too-short existence.

Arabella had wanted children; her physiology had denied her. She had wanted a long and peaceful life, but a cruel, consumptive illness had denied her both. Yet she had also wanted to be loved and, in his taciturn, ill-mannered way, Robert Knights had not denied her. He had never remembered her birthday or given Arabella any small token of his affection, but when he looked up from his labours as she passed the door of his workshop, his glance had always expressed his deepest devotion for her.

Miss Smy stood up and became aware that there was someone behind her.

"I hope I'm not intruding, Miss Smy."

It was Inspector Tranmer, his hat removed and held respectfully in his right hand. Miss Smy, still emerging from the tenderness of her thoughts, turned and coolly regarded him.

"I was about to call at your cottage, but as I passed the churchyard gate, saw that you were here. I heard about Mrs Knights. Consumption's a terrible thing, isn't it?"

Still Winifred Smy said nothing. There was so much she wished to tell him, especially standing over the grave of a woman whose husband had been accused by Tranmer himself of murder, but knew she could not trust herself to say the right thing.

Tranmer took a step forward and, with eyes to the ground, said, "I need to apologise."

"Why is that, Inspector?"

Tranmer now drew his hat up to his chest. "Have you ever lost someone whom you loved, Miss Smy?"

"I may have."

"If you have, and if you truly loved them, then you will know that the pain is almost more than your body can bear. You will know how your mind unravels, how all reason abandons you. You will also know the grief that consumes you entirely; the cruel dreams that fool you into thinking the person you love might still be alive. I have felt such darkness over these last years. You were right, I had thought of Suffolk as a new start. Different people and places to the ones my Annie and I had shared. But I still see her everywhere, Miss Smy. I know she's dead. I watched them lower her coffin. But I keep glimpsing her. She disappears around corners. From a distance, I am certain that

I see her walking towards me and then she, she...she becomes someone else."

Winifred Smy looked away, her lips tightly pressed together to assuage the way they trembled, unable to speak once more.

"May I tell you something else? After our last meeting, when you told me about the car at Aspall station and your conversation with Mrs Chevallier, I walked back to my room determined to ask to be taken off this case. I have blundered my way through this investigation and had even tried to get a man hanged for a crime that he did not commit. But to run away would have been another wrong on my part. I intend to make amends by Mr Knights and find the man who murdered Mr Carr-Pettiford. And I have come here today to tell you first."

Miss Smy brushed the earth from her hands and asked, "Would you care for tea, Inspector?"

Tranmer watched, with some admiration, the brisk efficiency of Winifred Smy as she set out the cups and saucers on the table.

"Do you always warm the pot?"

"Of course. Don't you?" She pushed the sugar bowl towards him and then poured out the tea.

"Thank you, Miss Smy. I need this."

The tea was satisfying and he returned the cup carefully to its saucer. "Miss Smy, I would like to set out what we now believe we know. Mostly facts and, if you will allow me, a few best guesses. May I do that?"

"Of course. I would find that useful."

"Mr Carr-Pettiford was discovered by the Kenton Junction Station Master at approximately 10.30 am on Tuesday 5th April.

We know he had been murdered and the murder weapon was...what was it again?"

"A screw gimlet."

"A screw gimlet. Thank you. He was last seen alive by the Station Master at Aspall, having left his car adjacent to the station premises. No one else was seen at the station but we know, from his diary, that Carr-Pettiford was due to see a man whose surname was indicated by the single letter 'B' at 10.15 am. Carr-Pettiford next appears at Kenton Junction Station, his body found, as I said earlier, by Station Master Whiting."

Miss Smy quickly interjected, "And let's not forget the incident with the burning jacket, which I am certain was cleverly arranged to distract Mr Whiting and the engine crew whilst, and I concede that this is pure supposition, the already dead body of Mr Carr-Pettiford was hastily installed in the station shelter."

Tranmer nodded his assent, before adding, "And the whole affair carefully orchestrated to make it appear as if it had been the murderous work of Robert Knights, even down to the careful planting of Mr Carr-Pettiford's wallet in the carpenter's workshop."

"Likewise, the deliberate selection of the screw gimlet as the murder weapon, Inspector. It is so irrevocably tied to the trade of a carpenter that we were meant to think it couldn't be anyone else."

"You're right. Knights' workshop is full of far more effective and anonymous murder weapons. Now, Miss Smy, is that everything we know?"

"Not quite, Inspector. I very recently spoke with PC Cornish. It seems that Carr-Pettiford has been in these environs before."

"Really?"

"Absolutely. Eleven years ago, he was selling shares in a railway that was meant to go from Kenton to Ipswich via Debenham. And do you know who bought most of those shares?"

Tranmer shook his head.

"Walter Bullingham. A coal haulier – amongst other things - in Debenham, who disastrously overstretched himself purchasing those shares and whose business never recovered. I have also heard since that Bullingham's disdain for that failed railway venture is now both vocal and violent."

Tranmer leaned forward. "Then Bullingham must be our Mr 'B'! We've found him!"

"Perhaps, Inspector. But there is still much work to do."

A loud rapping was heard on Miss Smy's front door before the agitated figure of PC Cornish ran into the kitchen.

"There you are, Inspector! I've been looken for you all over. Knights is dead! Killed himself! Poor blighter's been found hangen from a rafter in his own workshop. What's more – he's owned up to the murder. Look!"

Cornish handed the Inspector a grubby sheet of paper.

"I carnt live this lie anymore. My Arabella is ded and I lyed to her about not doing the murdur. I did it and I don't care who knows it now. Without hur there is nothing for me to live for. Dearest God forgive me."

Tranmer passed the note to Winifred Smy. "Well, I'll be blowed. Are we now to believe it was Knights all along?"

Miss Smy, attempting to hide the pain of the sudden news of Knights' death, was glad of the opportunity to scrutinise the message. She passed the note back to PC Cornish, her face a mask that refused to betray the emotions that now surged inside her.

"Remarkable."

Tranmer looked from Cornish to Miss Smy. "What's remarkable, Miss Smy?"

"It's remarkable that poor Robert Knights produced that confession before he died."

"I don't see what's remarkable about it. Many people leave notes before they kill themselves."

Winifred Smy, her face still devoid of any outward display of emotion, lifted her cup and sipped what remained of her tea, before asking, "Even those who are unable to read and write, Inspector?"

7

Two Visitors for Miss Smy

When Winifred Smy awoke just after dawn, she realised she was still fully dressed. She gradually recalled the events of the previous evening from the moment that PC Cornish had burst into her kitchen to say that Robert Knights had hanged himself. Inspector Tranmer had then quickly left her cottage with Cornish close behind. Only minutes later, several of the villagers had called on her, distressed by the news and desperately searching for information.

She slowly sat up on the bed and eyed her dishevelled appearance which she could now see in the dressing-table mirror. She remembered that the night before, she had gone to her room with the intention of preparing for bed but, instead, had decided to lie down for a short while, exhausted from the troubling events of the evening. Yet even the tumult of those thoughts had not prevented her from falling into a heavy, dreamless sleep.

The bell of All Saints church tolled the hour, and she decided to wash and change, determined to visit the workshop where Knights had spent his final hours.

Winifred Smy arrived at the Knights' house only to find it locked. Fortunately, she'd had the presence of mind to bring the key that Robert had entrusted to her so that she could call in to comfort Arabella in those last, awful weeks of her illness.

As she entered, she thought how hollow the house now seemed and sensed an invisible, oppressive presence hovering in every space she walked into. She went into the kitchen and pulled back the hessian cloth that had served as a curtain for the window, which was grimy from the soot of the kitchen fire. Hanging on a small nail to the side of the window hung the spare key to the workshop. She took it and walked outside and across the yard to the converted outbuilding that had served as Knights' place of work.

Pushing the door open, her senses were immediately assaulted by the smell of sawdust, but it was a familiar scent that she – like all Kenton villagers - had known since childhood. She pushed the door to and undid the buttons on her overcoat.

Knights' body had been taken away, as had the rope that had strangled him. In an unnerving way, everything still seemed grotesquely normal, almost as if Knights would at any moment come whistling into the building, asking her how her morning had gone or inquiring after the health of her mother.

As she was standing in the middle of the workshop imagining all that must have taken place the night before, her thoughts were suddenly interrupted by the creak of the door being opened. In a fleeting panic, she turned to see a woman whom she'd never met before. The woman was shocked to see Smy and instantly drew back as if to leave.

"Can I help?"

The woman, her entire upper body covered by a large, chequered shawl that she clasped to her chest, shook her head and kept her eyes to the ground.

"Are you a relative of Mr Knights? Or a friend, perhaps?"

Still, the woman said nothing. As Winifred Smy's eyes adjusted to the limited light in the workshop, she began to slowly make out the woman's features. She was tall in stature, with a wary, distrusting face and dark hair that was hardening into the grey of early middle age.

"I'm Winifred Smy, a friend of Robert and Bella."

The woman's frail body convulsed with the heave of a single sob before exclaiming, "I shouldn't have come!"

As Winifred Smy moved towards her, the mysterious woman shook her head and ran from the workshop. Smy quickly followed her only to see that she was already at some distance, running towards the direction of Kenton station.

The incident disturbed her. Who was the woman and why had she suddenly appeared in the Knights' property? She knew Robert Knights' family well - brothers, sisters, and several cousins - but this woman was completely unknown to her. It was at that very moment that a powerful thought arose in her mind about something she had noticed minutes earlier in the workshop but had failed to register. She immediately darted back inside and walked to Knights' workbench.

The first thing she saw was the large, half-finished wooden cross that Knights had obviously been preparing to mark Bella's grave. Graceful, intricate lines and flourishes had already been incised with devoted attention. Her eye then fell to a row of chisels that he would have been using, neatly arranged in order of size. Stepping back, she crouched down to look beneath the workbench. As she slowly raised herself again, she heard a familiar voice from the doorway.

"You know you really shouldn't be here, Miss Smy."

"I had to, Inspector. I knew this man well and, after the events of yesterday, I needed to feel close to him and Arabella."

Tranmer walked over to the bench and picked up the cross. "He was very skilled."

"He certainly was. He spent nearly all of his day producing the rude necessities that a carpenter must produce, but he was a craftsman through and through."

"Miss Smy, we both know that Mr Knights didn't commit suicide."

"Inspector, I am so relieved that you said that. As I said to you some days ago, we are dealing with someone who believes that the constabulary can be easily deceived. May I ask why you are so confident it wasn't suicide?"

"Oh, I've seen too many suicides. Enough to know that their faces are always much paler than someone who has been strangled."

"Strangled?"

"Without a doubt. The marks of injury on Knights' neck as he struggled are very apparent. And his complexion was that of a man who has died through ligature strangulation. The face is always much darker. Now that we have a little more light in this workshop, I would like to piece together exactly what happened yesterday."

"Exactly what I was doing just before you came in. Can I share my thoughts first? I would suggest that the attacker murdered Robert Knights as he was carving that cross for his wife. If you look beneath his workbench, you'll notice the long, agitated scuffs of his boots as he fought for his life."

Tranmer looked where Winifred Smy indicated before nodding his agreement.

"I can also tell you, Inspector, that although he was a fine craftsman, he was notoriously disorganised. The Robert Knights I knew would never have left those chisels and tools in such an orderly way. Whoever killed him tried to make this workbench appear neater so as not to draw anyone's attention to it. And as for the supposed suicide note, that was written by an educated person trying to make it appear as if it had been written by an uneducated hand. How would someone whose grammar and spelling are apparently so poor still manage to use capitals perfectly?"

"And what's more, Miss Smy, I find it very difficult to accept that he would spend so much time on producing this rather beautiful cross only to suddenly abandon it to take his own life."

"Inspector, a question for you. When I look at these chisels, I notice that one seems to be missing."

"I have that chisel, Miss Smy. I found it last night on the floor."

"And?"

"It was smeared with fresh blood. And I'm pretty certain it is the blood of our murderer."

Winifred Smy picked up one of the chisels, before adding, "And I have a strong suspicion that the murderer was someone he knew. Someone he knew rather well."

8

Was There Someone at the Door?

Inspector Tranmer carefully placed the wooden cross on the workbench and ruefully smiled. "That's a rather large claim to make. What makes you think Knights knew his killer?"

"It is only conjecture, I grant you, but I feel it in my bones that the last man Knights saw was someone he knew."

Tranmer sat down on the dead carpenter's stool and coolly observed Winifred Smy. "Then I am all ears. The stage is yours."

"On any normal day, Robert Knights would have these two large doors open, foul weather or fair. Often there would be a cart in this workshop or other objects of considerable size that he would be repairing. Whenever you entered this building, it would invariably have been through these doors. But you and I both know that on the day of his murder, a broken Robert Knights did not want to be disturbed. And why not? He was mourning his wife's untimely death and totally preoccupied with making this rather poignant cross for Arabella's resting place."

"With respect, Miss Smy, I'm not sure where all this is leading."

"Isn't it obvious? With the main doors closed, there can be only one other entrance into this workshop and that is the entrance you yourself used this morning."

Tranmer, arms folded high across his chest, wheeled his upper body around to view the door in question.

"You see, you were not the first visitor I had this morning. A woman, someone whom I have never met before, was here not long before you. A most perplexing meeting if I might say."

"A woman? In here?"

"Yes. And although, as I've said, she and I have never met, there was something familiar about her. Something I can't quite put my finger on."

"Perhaps she was the murderer? There are many instances..."

"...of returning to the scene of one's crime? No, I am certain she wasn't the murderer. She was dreadfully upset, though. The only thing she said was that she shouldn't have come here."

"Ah, that would be the woman I noticed hurrying ahead earlier. I saw you watching her as I was walking down the road."

"But you see, I had a warning that she had just entered, whereas you took me totally by surprise. What first alerted me to the woman's presence was the squeak of that door as it was opened."

Tranmer unfolded his arms and sat up, "But it didn't squeak when I came in."

"Of course not, because I had foolishly left it open in my hurry to return to the workshop."

"Now I see where you're going. Whoever came in that door last night would have announced their arrival by the noise it made when it was opened. Hang on, though. What if the door was already open, as it was for me?"

"I thought that too, but just try a little experiment for me, if you would be so kind. Stand by the door."

Tranmer did as he was told whilst Winifred Smy sat on the stool with her back to him.

"Now, Inspector Tranmer, as silently as you can, creep up behind me."

With the lightest of footsteps, Tranmer slowly and carefully walked across the first few yards of the floor, but each step was instantly betrayed by a creak of the wooden floorboards.

"Impossible. You can hear every blitherin' step."

"Exactly! Robert Knights would have been alerted the very moment his killer entered. But rather than set aside his work to talk to the intruder, we know he remained at his bench. So he must have known - and even trusted - the person who visited him last night. If Knights' killer was unknown to him, then there is not the slightest chance he would have ignored him and carried on working. Oh no, Inspector, the killer of Mr Knights was someone he not only knew - but knew well."

"And with Knights' back to the man, it would have been easy for our murderer to take the ligature out of this pocket, strangle him and then try to make it look like Knights had hanged himself. The rope would have easily covered up the marks that the strangulation had left."

"And, as you already know, whoever Knights' killer was, he may well be carrying a rather serious injury. If poor Robert Knights, in his desperate struggle, was able to injure his assailant with the chisel then that man might well make for a hospital or, at the very least, a refuge until he feels safe."

"Do you think Knights' murderer was a Kenton man?"

Winifred Smy thought for a while before replying, "I am not sure. I think not. And if he was badly hurt and came from this village, then we would soon find out. We are too huddled together for secrets to remain unknown for long, which I found out long ago to my own undoing."

Tranmer cocked his head to one side, finding such a remark incongruent with the rather severe demeanour of the woman he was looking at.

"Miss Smy, I really believe you have some interesting stories to tell."

"There is nothing remotely interesting about me, I assure you. And let's not allow ourselves to lose track of where our thoughts must go."

They both quickly became aware that a panicked voice was shouting from outside, "Inspector! Inspector Tranmer!"

They rushed from the workshop to find Edwin Cupper, a young farm labourer from Potash Farm, in an agitated state.

"Sir, are you the Inspector, Sir?"

"What is it, boy?"

"A body, Sir! We see'd a body! On the Aspall footpath! I said to Henry, I did, 'Look bor, tha'sa rum 'un, up ahead. That fare look loike someone's collapsed to me.' And we runned up and there he wuz. He wuz holden a rag. Blood all over it. On the rag and on his hands. We runned here and we were told the police inspector was hereabout."

After Cupper had conveyed to Winifred Smy exactly where the body was on the Aspall footpath, she asked him to fetch a cart from the farm. When it arrived, she directed the Inspector to sit up on the seat and, confidently taking the reins, immediately drove the two of them at speed towards and down Bellwell Lane. The Inspector had never been driven at such a ferocious pace before, and his unfamiliarity with a vehicle that had no suspension violently jolting across the irregular surface of a small country lane soon made him nauseous.

As the cart drew adjacent to a field gate, Smy skilfully pulled the horse up, and directed the Inspector – grateful that the transport ordeal was over - to open the gate for them. They then hurried across the width of the broad muddy field where, much to the dismay of Tranmer, his polished shoes sank into the damp Suffolk clay.

The body was easily seen from some distance and the Inspector slowed down and looked back towards Miss Smy. "Will you help me identify this man?"

"Of course."

But even before they had reached the body, Winifred Smy could see who it was. The distinctive elbow patches on the man's sleeves were easily made out as he lay face down in the grass.

It was only when the Inspector had reached the body that he realised that she had stopped some yards away.

"I thought you were going to help me identify him, Miss Smy?"

"I already know who that man is, Inspector. That man is – or was - Walter Bullingham."

9

Miss Smy Doesn't Tolerate Bad Manners

Winifred Smy wiped her hands on the small towel before reaching for her coat, draped over the back of the kitchen chair. At the foot of the stairs, whilst pulling on her gloves, she called up, "Mother! I have some errands to do. Try to sleep and I'll make some dinner when I return."

"Don't be long, Fred."

She had just closed the garden gate when she noticed a stranger standing at the junction by Kenton church. He looked up, raised his arm to attract her attention and shouted, "Excuse me!"

Winifred Smy took in his features as he quickly approached her. He was tall and his suit – which at first glance was clean and pressed - hung awkwardly from his thin frame, almost as if it sensed it was keeping undesirable company. His eyes were hooded in such a way that he instantly reminded Miss Smy of how a cobra might look after enjoying its prey. The man made a small bow, raised his hat and asked, "Have I the pleasure of the company of Miss Winifred Smy?"

"You are talking to Miss Winifred Smy. However, I am not in a position to confirm as to whether my company will be pleasurable or not."

The directness of her reply confused him at first, then his lips slid slowly back across a full mouth of white teeth and assumed a well-practised and insincere smile. "Quite. Allow me to introduce myself. The name's Manners. Nigel Manners Esquire. Framlingham Weekly News. Perhaps you take our paper, Miss Smy?"

"I do not. What is your business?"

Again, the brusqueness of her answer failed to puncture his inflated self-regard. She placed his age as probably early 30s and took a particular dislike to how his eyes appeared to be immovably fixed on her whilst his head and body clumsily swivelled around them.

"Miss Smy, a very good friend - a mutual friend if I may - has told me that you have some significant knowledge of the rather alarming incidents that have beset Kenton over these last weeks."

"And which friend is that?"

"Alas, propriety does not permit me to say."

"If we truly have a mutual friend, then there is no propriety to be compromised. And now that I have satisfied myself that this mutual friend is nothing but a fiction of yours, I will bid you good morning."

She turned sharply from the reporter and hurried on down Church Lane. But as she passed the entrance to the vicarage, Mr Manners was once again at her shoulder.

"Miss Smy, I fear that I might have irritated you. But please let me beg a very small amount of your time."

But she refused to stop, her face set firm in a determination to quit the wheedling intrusion of Mr Manners.

"Deeds not words!" he now shouted.

Miss Smy immediately halted; her shoulders dropped a little as she lowered her head.

"What did you say, Mr Manners?"

"'Deeds not words.' Mrs Pankhurst used those very words, I think. I have it on very good authority that you were a member of Mrs Pankhurst's Women's Social and Political Union. Not only a member but a very active participant in that organisation. Does the village of Kenton know that it has a prominent suffragette in its community, Miss Smy?"

With his trap sprung, Manners felt this was the moment to exert his full influence over her.

"Oh yes, Miss Smy. My newspaper colleagues in London seem to be awfully well acquainted with you. Not five years ago you were - and do please correct my facts if I am wrong here - protesting outside parliament alongside Mrs Pankhurst and many others, after the bill for women's suffrage was soundly rejected."

"It wasn't soundly rejected. A house composed entirely of incompetent males made sure that there wasn't sufficient time to debate it. They deliberately talked the bill out so that the legislation would never reach the statute book."

"Quite, quite. But you were also rather a jailbird as well, I am told."

Winifred Smy turned and walked slowly across to Manners, placing herself so close to him that he instinctively took a half-step back and leaned slightly away from her. "What, Mr Nigel Manners, is the real purpose of your visit? Have you come to gather news - or to peddle news?"

"With the greatest respect, I...ahem...think we might have got off to a rather bad start. I only want to make sure that I return to my editor with the facts about the Kenton murders."

"No, Mr Manners, you would like to return to your editor with a story, not the facts. You see, I know well how your 'profession' works. First, a reporter arrives at a story – one that is lurid, seedy and perfectly written to appeal to the many gullible people who read your paper – and then you sift through the evidence until you have one or two facts that give credence to the story. The remaining facts, the ones that you never needed to use, are simply discarded."

"I utterly resent that, Miss Smy. My intentions..."

"Your intentions, I warrant, are to move the recent events of this village from page 3 – which always accommodates the lewd and the local – to page 1, raising your professional standing substantially in the process."

"I resent that as well. You entirely misconstrue my motives."

Winifred Smy remained perfectly still, whilst the increasingly gauche movements of Manners' body continued to lurch around his immobile stare. She slowly leaned towards Manners, her eyes almost penetrating into his soul, stripping away the layers of mendacity and sophistry that wrapped tightly around his onion brain. He became increasingly unnerved, fearing what she might do next. But, to his surprise, she slowly stepped backwards and looked witheringly at him from his shoe-blacked boots up to the centre parting of his lank, greased hair. And then, in an instant, she had once more wheeled away from him, continuing her rapid walk towards Debenham.

But Nigel Manners was not to be deterred. After gathering his composure yet again, he was soon gaining on Winifred Smy.

"But Miss Smy!"

"Good morning, Mr Manners."

"But I have something to tell you. Something I know you'll want to know."

"I very much doubt it. Now go away or I shall report you to Constable Cornish."

"I know who she is!"

"I have no idea to whom you're referring, Mr Manners."

"Your mysterious lady. The one in Mr Knights' barn the morning after his murder. I know who she is!"

10

The Gossipers of Wilby

"Can I help you, Miss?"

The officer stood back from the police counter sensing that the irritation of the woman who had just walked in would be more difficult to handle than any pugnacious drunkard.

"I certainly hope so. Is Inspector Tranmer present?"

"And why would you need to see Inspector Tranmer?"

Winifred Smy bridled at the response and firmly placed her umbrella in front of her as if it was a weapon she might employ at any moment. She had battled her way up Market Hill through blustery rain to Framlingham Police Station and was in no mood for petty bureaucracy.

"Answer my question, please. Is Inspector Tranmer in this building?"

The officer pulled a large register towards him and started to flick casually through the pages. "Before I answer your question, Mrs...?"

"Smy. Miss Winifred Smy."

The officer looked up for the briefest moment; it was obvious that her name – if not her presence - was already known at the station.

"Before I answer your question, Miss Smy, I need to know why you need to speak with him."

"Then that answers my question, officer. He is in this building. I'm afraid that the issue is a private one, certainly one that I will not divulge in the reception of a police station. So, perhaps you would be good enough..."

A door at the end of the counter opened and Inspector Tranmer stood tall in its frame, pulling on his suit jacket.

"Thank you, Sergeant Audley. I am willing to see Miss Smy."

Tranmer opened a gate in the counter and beckoned her through. She followed him into a small room, unfurnished save for a table and two plain chairs.

"Please have a seat."

"I will not have a seat. I have come here to ask you why you have been sharing private conversations with the press. Yesterday I had the utter misfortune to be accosted by some seedy newspaper reporter who seemed to know more about what happened in Kenton than the East Suffolk Police!"

Tranmer pointed to a chair, "Please..."

"I tell you I will not sit down! Enlighten me, Inspector: is it police protocol to share private conversations with the likes of Mr Manners? Perhaps there was some little reward he put your way?"

"Miss Smy, I advise you to say no more!" Tranmer angrily replied. "Yes, I know Mr Manners and, yes, he was given some facts about the Kenton crimes, but not by me. Perhaps you would allow me to explain what happened?"

"It had better be a good explanation, Inspector."

Winifred Smy looked away, bristling with the depth of her anger.

"Miss Smy, when Robert Knights was found murdered and Bullingham's body found, a second inspector was assigned to the case. That is normal procedure in any murder enquiry. That inspector did something that many policemen do which is to use the advantage of certain contacts, and one of this inspector's closest contacts is Nigel Manners from the Framlingham Weekly News. You may resent these associations, but they exist, and such cooperation has been known to move many enquiries to a resolution."

"Are you telling me that the East Suffolk Police trades information with the local newspapers?"

"It is a custom that you will find the length and breadth of this land. I make no apology for it, but I was not the one that passed on the information to Mr Manners."

Tranmer pulled back a chair and sat down. Miss Smy resolutely remained standing. "Miss Smy, can I ask you what he told you that caused such obvious offence?"

"He told me that he had the name of the person who visited Robert Knights' workshop the morning after his death. I refused to listen and told him I had no interest in his tittle-tattle. I take it that what he said was true? You do know the name of the woman I saw in Robert Knights' workshop?"

"I'm afraid it is true. Her name is Hannah Palmer. A widow from the village of Wilby. Husband died young. No children, apparently."

"Palmer? That name means nothing to me. Are you certain we are talking about the same woman?"

The inspector sighed and looked away as if he was reluctant to continue the conversation. Miss Smy leaned her damp umbrella against the wall, removed her gloves and sat down. The quickness of her movements conveyed that she was still deeply irritated.

"Then, Inspector, I am at a loss. Tell me, how did Manners find this out?"

"My colleague, Inspector FitzAlan, shared some of the findings from the case with Mr Manners and let slip that this mysterious woman had suddenly appeared. Of course, men like Manners have a nose for a story and he soon tracked down who it might be. The first person he sought out was the Kenton Station Master. As you know, not many people use the Mid Suffolk train service and any new person on Kenton platform is soon noticed."

"What did Station Master Whiting tell him?"

"That a female passenger had a return ticket to Wilby. It doesn't take long for the likes of Nigel Manners to track down someone in such a small village like Wilby. Their Station Master soon corroborated the woman's journey."

"But whatever was her connection with Robert Knights? Was she a customer of his? Someone that he had carried out work for?"

"Miss Smy, I think we ought to leave it there. I have already told you much more than I should."

"Don't talk balderdash, man! Your colleague tells all to the press so, out of some respect to me, I feel I am entitled to hear all from you."

The Inspector looked wearily up at Miss Smy, "Do you mind if I have a cigarette?"

"Yes, I do mind. Your cigarette can wait. Are you covering something up, Inspector Tranmer? I believe you are. If there is something I need to know, I'd rather it came from you and not that viper, Mr Manners."

Tranmer spoke slowly and deliberately. "There was a connection but it's not one you're going to like. We interviewed Hannah Palmer and she told us nothing. But Manners inveigled himself with some of the gossips of Wilby and they were, shall we say, rather more forthcoming. Several months ago, Robert Knights was asked to repair damage done to the mediaeval bench ends at St Mary's Church in Wilby. From all accounts this seemed to take him longer than would normally be expected. Adjacent to the church is Hannah Palmer's cottage. It would appear that...Robert Knights and Hannah Palmer, if I may put it this way, took comfort in each other."

Winifred Smy's face slowly assumed a look of utter disbelief. "Robert Knights was seeing this woman?"

"I didn't want to have to tell you. I know that Mrs Knights and you were great friends."

"But...but it was known that he loved her. Arabella herself told me that he loved her so deeply. He did everything for her in those last months and weeks of her life."

"I am sure he did love her, Miss Smy. But sometimes two people do turn to each other for whatever reason."

Miss Smy sat in silence for some minutes. Tranmer, his hand steady on the edge of the table, knew not to speak. Presently, she reached for her gloves. "But this changes nothing, Inspector. We still have a murder to solve. Mr Knights and Mrs Palmer's betrayal has no bearing on what you and I do next."

"I agree. But there is something else I must share with you. You see, I have been instructed by Superintendent Freeman that he now considers the two murders to have been solved. That Walter Bullingham was the murderer of both Mr Carr-Pettiford and Mr Knights and that the wounds Bullingham sustained in the struggle in the carpenter's workshop were directly responsible for his own demise."

"What are you saying, Inspector?"

"I'm saying that Superintendent Freeman has announced that the case is now officially closed."

"Oh, is it? Then how do you explain that on the morning of Carr-Pettiford's death, Walter Bullingham was drawing money from his bank account in Ipswich? I learned this from a close employee of his in Debenham only yesterday morning."

"The case is closed, Miss Smy."

Winifred Smy sprang from her chair, opened the door of the interview room and shouted from the corridor, "Not for me, Inspector. Not for me."

11

A Quiet Lunch and a Melodic Hunch

The brisk broom of an impatient wind brushed away the remaining heavy clouds as if annoyed by their continuing indecision about whether to rain or not. A pleasing, clean breeze soon streamed across Kenton's open fields and eddied into the smallest corners and crevices of the farms, barns and cottages. Beneath the hedgerows, the butter-yellow faces of Lesser Celandine slowly revealed themselves, fragile fanfares sounding the return of the April sun.

With eyes fixed to the page of the sheet music sitting upon her piano, Winifred Smy was concentrating so hard on her playing that she failed at first to hear the knocking upon her cottage door. When the second series of raps coincided with a short *ritardando* in the music, she stopped, visibly irked by the unexpected interruption.

"Is that the door, Fred?"

"It is, Mother. I'll just answer it and then I'll make us some lunch."

"Who is it?"

She irritatedly muttered to herself, "I don't know yet. Telepathy isn't one of my talents."

She opened the door to Inspector Tranmer, who held out a woman's umbrella.

"Yours, I believe? You left it in the interview room."

Miss Smy looked nonplussed for some moments and then blurted out, laughing, "Yes, I believe it is."

She looked up at Tranmer's sou'wester which he had forgotten to remove. Embarrassed, he grabbed the incongruous hat and pushed it into a coat pocket.

"It's been raining," he explained. "It wasn't until I got to Monk Soham that the showers stopped. I cycled over, you see."

"Just to return my umbrella, Inspector?"

"Well, I...er..."

"Have you eaten lunch? I was just about to make something. You'd be very welcome."

Tranmer looked as if he was about to decline the offer, but then cheerfully returned, "I'd like that very much." He removed his coat and shook the dampness from it before stepping inside.

"Was that a Bach partita, Miss Smy?"

"Why, yes. I'm impressed. Do you know it?"

"We policemen do have lives and interests outside the force. An early one, if I'm not mistaken. The later partitas were more harmonically daring, I always think."

"Inspector Tranmer, I am going to have to radically change my view of you. Do you play?"

"A little. I took up the violin when I was much younger. That's how I met my wife. Both second violins. Just a little local orchestra. But you play very well, if I may say so."

"No, I don't, Inspector. I am rather more methodical than musical in my performance. But it pleases me to play, and my mother enjoys it."

Tranmer glanced awkwardly up at the ceiling, "Is your mother unwell?"

Winifred Smy didn't answer and hurriedly changed the subject. "Now let's see what I can get from the larder."

She placed what remained of a cold chicken pie on the table, followed by separate dishes of haslet and brawn. Smy then cut small pieces out of each and put them on another plate, spooning a little pickle onto the side. The plate was then set aside and she returned to the larder, soon re-emerging with a bowl containing a few eggs. "These were boiled only this morning. Please help yourself. I just want to take up Mother's lunch. Please do start. I won't eat very much."

When Smy returned, Tranmer was eating with gusto. "I've not had food this good for many a day. The room I rent, well, the landlady's cooking is well-meaning, but..."

"I'm glad you're enjoying it. It's only a small collation of some meats, but the farms serve us well. If you're not on duty, perhaps some beer?"

Winifred Smy pointed to a pewter flagon that stood on a high shelf, but Tranmer shook his head, "Not for me but thank you. You're very kind."

With lunch eaten and the dishes and cutlery cleared, Inspector Tranmer leaned back contentedly in the chair, drumming quietly on the table with the pads of his fingertips.

"I hope I am not speaking out of turn, Miss Smy, but do you know there is one thing that has always mystified me about you?"

"I may not be able to demystify you but do go on."

"Well, I assume that you were born and raised in Kenton, yet you don't sound like someone who was born and raised in Kenton. You've never once used a Suffolk phrase or expression and, when you speak, I can't detect any trace of a local accent."

Miss Smy removed her apron and considered her response. At length, after removing two or three tired-looking wildflowers from a small arrangement on the window ledge, she turned to Tranmer. "Have you ever heard of Bernard Shaw, Inspector? Mr George Bernard Shaw?"

"The playwright? I've heard of him, but that's all I'm afraid."

"I had the pleasure, when I was working in service in London, to overhear a discussion between him and another guest at a rather large house party. During that conversation he said that it was impossible for an English man to open his mouth without making some other English man despise him. I knew what he meant. As soon as one speaks one betrays one's class - and you are forever damned by it."

"Are you saying you changed your accent so people would think better of you?"

"I am telling you exactly that. When one is seeking employment, you make the choice to speak either as a housemaid or a housekeeper. As you well know, there is a world of difference between both positions, not least financially, and I chose to replicate the demeanour and accent of a housekeeper. I'm not proud of it because I love Kenton and I deeply love Suffolk. I felt a sense of betrayal in what I did, but I did it all the same. I admire the fact that you, however, have chosen to speak authentically."

"Oh, I wouldn't know how to sound any different. I am who I am, Yorkshire through and through, accent and all."

Satisfied with her answer, the Inspector paused and looked down as his finger traced the slight ridge of a small knot of wood in the kitchen table.

"You have something else on your mind, perhaps, Inspector?"

"Indeed, I do. I'm not on duty, Miss Smy. Your umbrella was, I do admit, a convenient excuse for me to call on you. You see, I've been troubled since our meeting yesterday. Very troubled. I need to speak to you candidly, but what I want to share with you must remain only between ourselves."

"You intrigue me."

"Perhaps, but I need your word that this conversation will be in the strictest confidence."

"You have my word. Excuse me, a moment."

She stood up and softly pushed the kitchen door closed.

"My mother may be ill, but she can hear a wren's wing flap in Stradbroke."

Tranmer briefly smiled, before continuing, "Yesterday, when I spoke with you at the police station, I did so as an officer of the law. When the superintendent instructs me that a case is closed, then I must obey my superior officer. You must understand that?"

Winifred Smy nodded.

"But all through this case, these murders and everything, you have constantly reminded me that there are, shall we say, inconsistencies. Inconsistencies that imply that Mr Carr-Pettiford's death was not at the hands of Walter Bullingham."

"I agree."

"Miss Smy, I no longer doubt that Bullingham and Knights' deaths can now be accounted for. But the death that preceded these most unfortunate events has not been resolved."

"I am gratified to hear you say that. I am sorry if I appeared a little too...agitated in my manner yesterday, but all this has vexed me most deeply. Some matters have never been resolved to my satisfaction. The jacket that coincidentally..." Miss Smy raised an eyebrow as she said this, "was set alight on the morning the body was found..."

"To divert the attention of everyone?"

"Absolutely. That was done deliberately. To my knowledge, the man whom Carr-Pettiford was supposed to be meeting on the morning he was murdered has never made himself known. Why has he not come forward? And, as I told you only yesterday, Bullingham was some fifteen miles away in Ipswich at the time of the murder, making a withdrawal at his bank. Oh yes, Inspector, I am convinced that the man who murdered Charles Carr-Pettiford is still at liberty."

Tranmer reached into an inside pocket and took out a small piece of paper, which he handed to Miss Smy.

"This is the London address of Charles Carr-Pettiford's residence. He was a bachelor by all accounts. My colleagues in London have spoken with his two servants but report that they had very little to say. I'm not convinced. I would have preferred to talk to them myself but, as the investigation is officially closed, I am not permitted to do so. However, such a proviso does not apply to you."

"What could I possibly find out, Inspector? It's a long way for what might prove to be very little."

The Inspector walked over to the piano, sat on the small stool and studied the score that sat on the music rack.

"Do you know what I love most about Bach, Miss Smy?"

"Enlighten me."

"It is the hidden melodic lines. When you first hear Bach, the beauty of his melodies takes your breath away. But when you return to the same music and listen more deeply, what you start to notice are hidden lines of melody, so cleverly weaved inside the work that you have to strain to tease them out. When I was first assigned this case, all I could notice was the obvious melody. I admit I blundered somewhat badly there, and you were right to try and make me aware of it. And now that I have been pulled away from this investigation, I start to see how little time I gave to the subtleties, the hidden clues that may have been there all the time."

"And Carr-Pettiford's servants hold the key to one of those hidden melodies?"

"I am certain of it. It's probably just a copper's intuition, but my instinct tells me that they might be able to help. So, will you go to London to see them?"

"Oh, you just try and stop me, Inspector Tranmer. Now, shall we have tea?"

12

Miss Smy Tries to Play her Part

As the fields outside the train window passed from those of Suffolk to Essex, without any discernible difference in shape or appearance, Winifred Smy felt the dawning realisation that, as she had told Inspector Tranmer earlier in the week, the trip to Charles Carr-Pettiford's London home would probably be a fruitless one. She had yet to think of a pretext for even being there. The servants who remained in the house would not know her and the first and last time that she had seen Carr-Pettiford was when his slumped, lifeless body occupied the corner of the waiting area at Kenton Junction.

Perhaps she could alight at Colchester and simply retrieve what would usefully remain of the day when she eventually returned home? She turned this option over in her mind and found herself drawn to and repelled by it in equal degrees. But the injustice of three deaths within her own parish boundary – and the unresolved details that surrounded them - tipped the scales in her mind and she realised that, if nothing else, the quest might yield nothing or everything.

She dipped her hand into her small bag and took out the note that Inspector Tranmer had given her the day before. In neat, sloping handwriting it read:

Charles Carr-Pettiford Esq.

18 Mecklenburgh Square

London

What she had not revealed to Tranmer as she looked at the address was that she knew the square well, and the name immediately brought back the animated conversations and arguments that ricocheted around the walls of number 44 Mecklenburgh Square, home to the People's Suffrage Federation. She fondly recalled her time laboriously addressing envelopes to raise support for the right for women to vote, seated at times by the lowly and the elevated, all bent on a cause that united them.

Liverpool Street Station was noisy and filled with a thousand odours that immediately assaulted her senses. Living in Suffolk, where its familiar scents were borne through the village on a steady sou' westerly, she had forgotten the dizzying range of aromas that London offered, from the delicately scented perfume of a woman of means, through to the reeking stench of a local tannery.

Remembering that Russell Square station had opened only three or so years previously and, after asking a guard the best route to reach it, she joined the heaving bustle of the great and good of the unsleeping metropolis to make her way there. From

Russell Square station, it was a short walk of 10 minutes before she turned into Mecklenburgh Square itself, which was exactly as it was when she had last seen it; both grand and dowdy, like a frumpy uncle who had socially fallen from high.

Carr-Pettiford's home was more modest than many on the square, yet still belied an elegance with its chequerboard steps and tiles that led up to a wide front door, capped by an arched fanlight. Looking up, she could see a small, ornate balcony that ran before the two upper windows of the first storey. One window was open a little, so she surmised that someone must be in.

She firmly sounded the door knocker twice before stepping back and gathering herself for the charade she knew she must play. Behind the door, she heard an inner lock released and the unmistakable rattle of a chain being drawn back. It opened slowly to reveal a small woman dressed in a servant's attire. She had obviously removed her apron moments before as Smy could see it folded on the hall table. The woman took in the figure of Winifred Smy, her eyes narrowing in suspicion.

"Good morning, Ma'am. Can I help you?"

Smy's face immediately brightened as she endeavoured to arrange her features in as friendly a way as she could.

"I'm terribly sorry to disturb you, especially in light of your recent and most terrible loss, but I am from the Mid-Suffolk Light Railway company. The name's Berry. Miss Edith Berry. Before Mr Carr-Pettiford met his dreadful end he asked, as he knew I was coming up to London, if I could pick up a letter that he had signed and left in his study. May I collect it?"

"I've seen no letter in his study. Why it's as tidy as can be. If he'd left a letter on his desk, then I'd 'ave seen it."

"That's most peculiar. He was insistent it was in his room. But I seem to recall, he didn't specifically mention where he'd left it in his study. I've come such a long way and I really must have it as it's important that I take it to the bank in Ipswich."

"An 'e never mentioned a 'Miss Berry' before. Where did you say 'e was when he told you?"

"Why, at Mr Chevallier's house in Aspall."

The mention of the Chevallier name immediately removed the wariness of the housekeeper and she opened the door wide and beckoned Winifred Smy to enter.

"I'm sorry, Ma'am. There's been such comings and goings here with the police and whatnot that I'm fed up to the back teeth with nosy strangers. Would you like tea?"

"Oh yes, very much."

"If you go into the room on your left, I will not be long."

Smy removed her gloves and hat, unbuttoned her coat, and sat in the comfortable room. It was tastefully furnished, and she could see that whoever had arranged the decoration of the room had done so with considerable flair. Generous light filled the space and only the occasional sound of horses' hooves from the square outside broke the silence.

The housekeeper returned and carefully transferred the cup, saucer, and teapot to a small table adjacent to Miss Smy.

"So, you knew Sir, did you?"

"Mr Carr-Pettiford? No, I'm afraid only a little. Mr Chevallier is the one I knew best. I believe he met with Mr Carr-Pettiford and the other directors in London most of the time."

Winifred Smy was feeling keen pangs of guilt and was coming to hate every moment of the pretence. She tried to remind herself of the cause she was serving but still found it didn't assuage her growing feelings of self-disgust.

"Was he a nice man?"

The housekeeper paused for a moment and looked through the window to the square's private garden outside, before answering, "He was 'is own man. He 'ad 'is ways. I didn't ask questions and neither did my 'orace."

"Horace?"

"Sir's butler and my 'usband. He looked arter us and we looked arter 'im. Still looking arter 'im, what with all these busybody police and the like."

Winifred Smy could bear the deceit no longer and she decided that this was no way to continue. She finished her tea and placed the cup and saucer back on the table.

"You've been very kind, but I really should be going. Thank you for your kind hospitality. The tea was extremely refreshing."

"Aren't you forgettin' something?"

"Am I?"

"That letter. You said it was in the study. Let me take you there."

Smy felt that she couldn't now refuse and told herself that all she had to do was to affect a cursory glance around Carr-Pettiford's study before pretending that it must have already been posted to the bank. Dutifully, she followed the servant into Carr-Pettiford's large study. It strangely resembled a solicitor's office with the heavy desk placed squarely in the centre of the room, with books – some real and some just spines in fake panels – lining two sides of the room. A heavily curtained window looked out onto the rear garden area.

"Can I leave you 'ere for a moment, Ma'am? I just need to take those tea things back to the kitchen."

"Of course; I'm sure I won't be long."

With the housekeeper now out of the room, Winifred Smy first bided her time by looking at the few, unremarkable paintings on the walls. Then her eye noticed a crumpled letter that was half-hidden behind a brown leather briefcase. She picked it up, telling herself that she would hand it over to the housekeeper as soon as she returned, but found that she could not deny herself slowly teasing it open to read. She walked to the window to read the letter more easily. What she saw forced her to gasp in surprise.

"Oh, my good Lord. I know this handwriting. I know this handwriting very well."

13

An Unlikely Pact

Winifred Smy watched the drab buildings of East London slip past her train window. She felt inside her bag once more to reassure herself that the crumpled letter she had found on the floor of Carr-Pettiford's study was still there. She knew it was the breakthrough she had been looking for and was now eager to return to Kenton.

She recalled how, earlier that morning, she had experienced great moments of self-doubt, sufficient to make her consider whether to alight at the next station and return to Suffolk. But now everything about the baffling murders was falling into place, although she still felt perturbed by the direction – and the person – to whom that evidence now pointed.

Having been pleased to find a compartment to herself, she was dismayed to hear the door opening as a man entered from the train corridor.

"Why, Miss Smy!"

She glanced up at the interloper and could not contain her disappointment as she quickly recognised who it was. "Ah, Mr Manners. You surprised me."

"I saw you getting on at Liverpool Street and was determined that I should sally forth back to Suffolk in the delightful company of your very good self. Of course, I am being rather presumptive – but it would turn this tiresome journey into something much more felicitous if you would allow me to share this compartment with you."

She wanted to decline Manners' company – and the avalanche of bloated sentences she was sure would follow - but found that her own sense of decorum wouldn't allow her to do so. She nodded her assent with the rictus smile she hoped would not betray her true feelings.

Manners seated himself and lay his case, hat and newspaper on the seat next to him, all done whilst he continued to look at Miss Smy, as if his two eyes were strangely independent of his body. Leaning forward in a conspiratorial way, he lowered his voice and asked, "Were we visiting friends, Miss Smy?"

"I'm sorry?"

"In London. Were we visiting friends?"

"No. And you?"

"Oh, just calling on an old chum. Another newspaper fellow. Jolly useful contact. Excellent lunch."

Manners leaned back into his seat. Miss Smy looked out of the window once more, hoping that he might take to his newspaper, but secretly knowing that he wouldn't. Before many seconds had passed, her slim hope of a quiet journey was dashed.

"So, it was Walter Bullingham all along, eh? Remarkable. Quite remarkable."

Smy knew that Manners was spinning a web to catch her, yet she persevered in trying to avoid becoming ensnared in his conversation.

"What do you think of Russell Square station, Miss Smy? Still looks quite new, I think. And very handy for so many places: Fitzrovia, British Museum, Mecklenburgh Square..."

The mention of Mecklenburgh Square caused Smy to involuntarily look from the passing buildings back to Manners, who met her eyes with a knowing look.

"How did you know I was at Russell Square, Mr Manners? Have you been following me?"

Manners guffawed before responding, "Miss Smy, you do me a great disservice. I was on the train already and saw you as it pulled into Russell Square station. You were, I think, on the carriage adjoining mine. I saw you enter."

"Why did you specifically mention Mecklenburgh Square?"

"Oh, just a lucky guess, but I do hear that it is a popular area for *la femme militante,* if you follow my meaning. I merely surmised that you might have been visiting some old acquaintances from your own particular feminine regiment."

Winifred Smy took an instant dislike to the sneering tone Manners voice assumed when referring to her past attachment. She decided that she would, again, keep her counsel. But, true to form, Manners would not let it rest.

"I also do believe that Mecklenburgh Square was the residence of the unfortunate fellow who was murdered in Kenton. Anyway, it's very wrong of me to assume that that was the purpose of your visit. I'm sure that it wasn't the case at all. Is that not so, Miss Smy?"

"Mr Manners, I am beginning to find your impudent conjecture rather objectionable. If there is a question that you want to ask me, then I implore you to do so directly. You may find it elicits a good deal more candour from me."

"Pray tell me, are we still dallying with the law, Miss Smy? Still pursuing our enquiries, perhaps? I'm always looking for a story. How about, 'Meet Suffolk's Beautiful Lady Detective'. It would make a rather good feature, don't you think?"

"Is it Ipswich you change at for Framlingham, Mr Manners? I do hope so as I can enjoy the rest of my journey without your insufferable questions. Perhaps you will ease the rest of my journey by allowing me to read your newspaper. Would you mind?"

Manners smiled weakly and handed her his paper. Luckily for Miss Smy, it was a broadsheet, and she wasted no time in opening it up to its full height and width so as to screen herself from Manners. The journey continued in a strained silence but, just as the train was pulling out of Manningtree station, Miss Smy suddenly lowered one corner of the paper and said, "Mr Manners, I need to ask you to do something."

Manners was caught momentarily off-guard. "Of course," he replied, before artfully adding, "But I may have a favour to ask in return."

"As long as it is not a dubious request then I will endeavour to honour it. I will speak plainly. The revelation that Robert Knights was visiting Hannah Palmer in Wilby caused me some considerable distress. I take comfort that his wife Arabella went to her grave ignorant of the details of the whole tawdry matter. In all of this I have often returned to the conviction that Mr Knights' companion..." (Manners smiled at the tactful euphemism) "...is somehow familiar. I would be very grateful if you, someone with a penchant for uncovering what many would prefer to remain hidden, could gather more information about her."

"And I would then take what I find to the police?"

"No. You will convey what you discover to me only. Besides, as you well know, the police have no further interest in this investigation."

Manners pondered the request, his thin hands held before him as if he was at prayer. "Then I will do it. But now I have something I would like to ask of you."

"And that is?"

"I think you know who killed Mr Carr-Pettiford, and it wasn't Walter Bullingham. When you uncover his killer, I want to be there."

It was now Miss Smy's turn to think through the request. With a certain deliberation, she answered, "If I should find myself in a position to identify the real murderer, then I will alert you in good time. Thank you for your newspaper."

It was a tired Miss Smy that, some considerable time later, alighted at Kenton Junction. She was just adjusting her hat before the walk homeward when she was greeted by Station Master Whiting.

"Good journey, Miss Smy?"

"Yes, thank you. I'm very glad I've seen you. I know we've already spoken about this, but may I ask you something else about the day you found Mr Carr-Pettiford?"

"Oh, that. I can't think what else yew'd want to know. I told the Inspector everything that happened."

"Yes, I know, but I'd like to ask you about the time just before you found the body. When you were alerted to a burning jacket at the side of the train."

"That was a rum old dew, right enough. Can't think how it even got there. It wasn't there before the train from Aspall arrived."

"So how did you know about it? It was on the opposite side to the platform, wasn't it?"

"It certainly was. Someone shouted out the window. 'Fire!' they hollered. Course, old Bloom, the fireman, looked out from his engine and saw it. 'Cood blaarst me,' said he, 'there's suffen burning under that carriage!' We all runned round to it as fast as we could to put it out. Rummin it wuz, and no mistake."

"Who shouted out of the window to tell you? Did you recognise his voice?"

"Oh, it wasn't a man's voice that shouted. It was a woman's voice. 'Fire!', she shrick, everyone heard it."

"Are you certain?"

"As certain as I'm standen here before yew."

"I now have the murderer," she whispered to herself, before turning briskly for home.

14

The Gathering on the Platform

The devil still hovered high and menacing over the village of Kenton and, from his lofty aerial perch, he could see six figures making their way towards Kenton Junction; this would be - for one of them - their own final date with destiny. Two were to arrive by train, whilst three trudged towards the station along the Eye Road. The last was cycling in his own distinctive manner up Bellwell Lane, having just mounted his cycle again after failing to summon the necessary energy to surmount the long, steady rise from Debenham.

It was Winifred Smy who arrived first. She checked her wristwatch; it was ten minutes past ten. Inspector Tranmer appeared next at the crossing gate and, seeing Miss Smy already on the platform, raised his hat to her.

"I wasn't sure if you'd come," she said as he reached her.

"I'm not certain why you've asked me."

The wind tugged and pulled in different directions across the open station, snatching at coats and trousers, hems and hats, like a child desperate for a parent's attention.

"Your message was, dare I say, a little cryptic, Miss Smy?"

"Perhaps, but I am genuinely delighted that you are here. I just hope I will not have wasted your valuable time." She put her hand on his sleeve, part reassuring and part wanting to be reassured. His face softened at the gesture.

"So, what happens now?"

"We must wait. That's what happens now."

A clatter of metal announced the arrival of PC Cornish as he threw his bike resentfully down on the platform.

"Morning, Sir. Miss Smy. I thought I was going to be wholly late. That Bellwell Lane is going to be the death of me. Cood blaarst me! Who is that?"

On the opposite platform stood Hannah Palmer, the woman from Wilby that Robert Knights had been secretly seeing. Appearing as if she'd suddenly materialised out of thin air, she stood defiantly hatless and motionless, with the probing fingers of the wind tossing her brown hair across her mask-like face.

"Will you join us, Miss Palmer?" shouted Winifred Smy across the rails. Reluctantly, Hannah Palmer walked down towards the road, crossed the track, and slowly approached the small group.

Tranmer looked anxiously at Miss Smy. "Is this the..."

"More of that presently, Inspector. You see, I need to take the four of us right back to the beginning."

Tranmer was adamant, "Not again. Surely we've turned all of that over too many times now?"

"This was where you and I first met, Inspector. I had a parcel to leave with Mr Whiting, the Station Master, when I was surprised to see so many from the village standing around the opposite platform. I walked up only to find you, the Superintendent and PC Cornish all in the waiting area. That was when I also saw the body of Mr Charles Carr-Pettiford."

"Ah, the screw gimlet. You pointed out what the murder weapon was."

"No great revelation on my part but, in an instant, three things struck me as rather odd."

"Three things, Miss Smy?"

"Yes, PC Cornish. The first was the hat. If this man had been murdered in this waiting area, the struggle would have been violent and desperate. And yet, there he was neatly slumped on a chair with his hat perfectly in place."

"Well, now you come to mention it..." mumbled the policeman.

"Oh, but I do mention it. The person who had assaulted him had placed the hat neatly back upon his head. Is that not so, Mrs Palmer?"

Hannah Palmer shot an angry glance at Winifred Smy.

"And what also struck me as decidedly odd, was that there had been no indication of any struggle, either visibly or audibly. Surely, if a man had been fighting for his life, Station Master Whiting or his two assistants would have heard? After all, Inspector, your first suspicion was that Robert Knights had killed him before the train had arrived."

PC Cornish sniffed and pushed back his helmet, nodding in agreement with her logic.

"I was recently in Mr Carr-Pettiford's residence in London and, before I left, I asked the housekeeper what had become of his clothes. She told me that they had been removed so that he might be buried in something more becoming. But his coat and shoes had been returned. I asked the housekeeper if I might see the shoes and, after some persuasion on my part, she assented. Sure enough, both shoes had easily discernible scuff marks on their heels, as if Mr Carr-Pettiford had been dragged backwards across a hard, concrete surface."

"From the train carriage to that waiting area?" said Tranmer.

"Exactly. You and I had already concluded that the poor man was dead before the train arrived at this station. All it took, to transfer him from the train carriage to the shelter without anyone seeing, was a simple diversionary tactic."

"The burning jacket," confirmed the Inspector. "Hung out of the window, covered in petrol and set alight and dropped on the opposite side of the train. And then, with everyone distracted, and making sure that no one else was around, the murderer dragged the body into the shelter and made it look as if the man was just sleeping."

PC Cornish interrupted, "You said there were three things, Miss Smy?"

Once more she looked at Hannah Palmer, who continued to observe Miss Smy with an insolent stare. "The screw gimlet, Constable. Robert Knights may not have been able to read or write, but he was not a stupid man. Why would anyone use such a recognisable tool of their trade and then leave that weapon at the murder scene? They would be suspected instantly. Is that not right, Mrs Palmer?"

"How would I know?" Miss Palmer snapped back.

"Quite. But let's not lose our line of thought now..."

"Stand back! Train from Aspall and Thorndon!" Percy Whiting, the Station Master, strode purposefully out on to the platform, reassuringly glanced at his pocket watch and peered at the engine and carriages that had stopped at the far crossing gate. Fireman Bloom stepped down from the engine and opened the two gates across the Eye Road. Eventually, the train hauled its carriages slowly along the length of the platform and, with a painful hissing and squealing of brakes, it came to rest.

Inspector Tranmer had just turned back towards Miss Smy when he noticed a carriage door being opened, and a woman – tall and large of frame – stepping out before heaving the train door to with a loud report that rose above the din of the idling engine.

"Ah, I've been waiting for you," said Miss Smy.

15

Someone Finds There's the Devil to Pay

There stood Elizabeth Bullingham, who, seeing a small group already assembled, looked a little confused. "You said you needed to see me, Miss Smy? Said it was urgent? Well, it better…"

It was only then that she noticed Hannah Palmer was also present.

"What are you doing here?"

"Don't you talk to me, Bess. Not after what your Walter did to my Robert!"

"I don't know what yew're talken' about. Anyway, he wasn't your Robert," snarled Elizabeth Bullingham.

Inspector Tranmer appeared a little surprised and looked from one woman to another for answers.

Miss Smy said, "Let me explain, Inspector. After I briefly met Miss Palmer in Robert Knights' workshop - the day after he had been murdered - you will recall that I told you I was certain that there was something familiar about her. Yet, for the life of me, I couldn't think what it was. And then, thanks to a very persistent newspaper man whom you know well, I discovered they were..."

"Sisters?" Elizabeth Bullingham shouted. "And what of it? What's your game here?"

"Nobody knows this line like Mrs Bullingham. Every Tuesday she takes the train from Aspall Station to Wilby to visit her sister, Hannah."

"And that's a crime, Miss Smy? Seeing my sister?"

Miss Smy checked herself and calmly reached into her bag. "I believe this belongs to you." She handed a crumpled note to Elizabeth Bullingham.

"Where did you get this?" she demanded.

"I found it in Mr Carr-Pettiford's study. I assume that he had scrunched it up and thrown it to one side in anger."

Tranmer stepped forward, "I don't understand."

"Oh, I do, my dear Inspector." But it wasn't Miss Smy who had answered him. From behind a large and high mound of coal sacks some yards from the group, stepped out Nigel Manners. He stood - still unable to keep his thin frame from involuntarily shifting - before them all: Miss Smy, Inspector Tranmer, Hannah Palmer, Elizabeth Bullingham and PC Cornish.

"Some of you already know that in 1899, Mr Charles Carr-Pettiford visited Debenham, selling shares in a new train project. One that would supposedly connect that village with Ipswich and all points beyond. Walter Bullingham not only bought many of those shares, but he also invited Carr-Pettiford to his home. It soon became common knowledge in the village that Carr-Pettiford and Mrs Bullingham went on to see quite a lot of each other."

"That's a lie!" shouted Elizabeth Bullingham.

"And it was also rumoured," continued Manners, "that Walter Bullingham was not the father of Elizabeth Bullingham's son."

"How dare yew say such things! How dare you drag our family name through the midden. No one has any proof..."

"That letter you are holding is the proof, Bess." said Miss Smy. "In that letter you remind Mr Carr-Pettiford that he is the father of your son, not Walter Bullingham. And that if he doesn't continue with the payments, you will share that secret with the world, shaming him and bringing down the disapproval of all society upon his head. Your husband never killed Mr Carr-Pettiford because on that morning he was in a bank in Ipswich drawing down on funds that magically appeared in his account every month. But the last letter you sent to Charles Carr-Pettiford – the very one you are holding now – was the last straw."

Mr Tranmer quickly interjected, "So that's who the 'B' was in his appointment diary. Not Walter Bullingham – but Bess."

"Yes, the 'B' was Bess Bullingham, and I would propose she received a letter in reply from Mr Carr-Pettiford telling her, despite her threats to publicly expose him, that he was keeping with his decision to halt the payments to her and her husband. She, no doubt, soon learned of Carr-Pettiford's imminent arrival at Aspall Hall and from that moment, began her plans to exact her terrible revenge."

"But if Carr-Pettiford had already made his mind up to stop the payments, why would he agree to see Mrs Bullingham?"

"Oh, only Bess would know the answer to that. It would be easy enough to contrive an excuse for the fact that they must meet. A promise from Mrs Bullingham to return some incriminating letters, perhaps? Whatever it was, it lured him to Aspall Station to keep his grim appointment."

PC Cornish, feeling that matters were moving to a head, hurriedly restored his helmet to its official place before asking, "But where does Knights fit into all this?"

"Mrs Bullingham knew that Robert Knights was in a relationship with her sister and deeply resented the fact," said Miss Smy. "Mr Manners had learned of arguments a couple of villagers had overheard from Mrs Palmer's house, with Bess telling her sister that she was still vulnerable after her husband's death and Knights was just taking advantage of her."

"So now," added Inspector Tranmer, "she had the perfect opportunity to deal with two grievances, not only to take out her revenge on Mr Carr-Pettiford, but to arrange it so that it was Robert Knights who was implicated and arrested."

Nigel Manners picked up the narrative. "A little investigating of my own soon established that Knights had carried out some work at Walter Bullingham's house the previous week. Apparently, one or two of his tools had gone missing..."

"Including a screw gimlet?"

"Exactly, Inspector," answered Miss Smy, "and then, in between Aspall and this station, in a carriage which all her previous journeys to her sister had assured her would be empty, she murdered the hapless Carr-Pettiford using Knights' own work tool. And with the deed done and the body dragged to the waiting area, all she needed to do afterward was to find the moment to plant Carr-Pettiford's own wallet somewhere on Knights' premises. Miss Smy tells me it was a woman's voice that shouted the alarm about the burning jacket, not a man's voice. The only man in that train carriage was a dead man."

"Hang on there, Mr Manners, before I get wholly lost. What's Walter Bullingham's involvement? Why did he kill Robert Knights?" PC Cornish was keen to keep up with the rapidly unfolding tale.

"Oh!" said Manners. "With Knights released and his name cleared, one can only imagine that Elizabeth Bullingham told her husband that he might emerge as the chief suspect. After all, it was well known in Debenham that he had an axe to grind with the railway company. He never missed an opportunity to let people know how angry he was with the directors who had taken his money and then abandoned the line to Debenham."

Miss Smy added, "I think Walter Bullingham could sense that the game was up. As for Mrs Bullingham, if anyone found out about her connections to the murdered man, then she would also have been of great interest to the police. Perhaps Mrs Bullingham tipped him off that..."

"Tipped him off!" roared Elizabeth Bullingham, "Tipped him off! That fool? I told 'im, if he doesn't make it look like suicide then one of us is for the drop! All he needed to do was to make it look convincen. But he couldn't even do that."

"And that is why you wrote the suicide note, isn't it, Mrs Bullingham?"

Bess Bullingham stared down at Miss Smy. "How d'yew know I wrote any suicide note?"

"Because it exactly matches the same handwriting on the letter I found in London from you to Mr Carr-Pettiford. The suicide note was written by your hand, Mrs Bullingham. Oh, you tried to make it look like it was written by someone who had very little education, but the style of the handwriting was unmistakably yours. The oversight on your part was that Robert Knights was completely illiterate."

Whilst Winifred Smy had been speaking, Elizabeth Bullingham had started to step slowly backward down the platform and, noticing that the train to Worlingworth was already pulling away, grabbed at a handle and yanked open a carriage door. The speed of the train was picking up and Mrs Bullingham now tried to throw herself into the moving carriage.

"Don't you dare!" screamed Hannah Palmer, who ran down the platform and threw herself at Elizabeth Bullingham, trying to pull her away from the carriage. But, in the brief struggle, Elizabeth Bullingham's sleeve had become caught in the door hinge and, losing her balance, she was turned over on to her back.

Hannah Palmer lost her grip on her sister's dress and fell to her knees, helpless as she watched the struggling woman. "Elizabeth!" she cried out.

Despite Elizabeth Bullingham's frenzied attempt to haul herself back up with her free hand, the sleeve remained caught and soon she was being cruelly dragged along the platform. Unaware of the slaughter and the screams that were behind him, the engine driver continued to increase the speed, and the helpless body of Elizabeth Bullingham was finally sucked under the wheels of the carriage frame.

Hannah Palmer stared at the departing train in shock, with Miss Smy quickly burying her sobbing head into her shoulder, not allowing her to see the gruesome scene that was still unfolding on the track. A few minutes later, at some point near Flemings Hall, the engine disgorged its bloody trophy and it fell to a passing farm labourer to chance upon the discarded body.

PC Cornish removed his hat and sat disconsolately on the platform. Manners, Tranmer and Miss Smy exchanged the briefest of glances.

Presently, Winifred Smy found Percy Whiting and asked him to look after Mrs Palmer, who was now numb with grief.

"I never thought it would be a woman, Miss Smy. Not for a moment." said Tranmer.

Miss Smy angrily turned on the Inspector. "Why not? Are we still only 'the angel in the house' to you? Do we not share the same capacity to love and hate? To be kind and cruel? To feel generous or bitterly resentful? Resentful to the point that we might spin towards some terrible revenge. If a man has these potentialities within him, why not a woman?"

Rather than reply, Tranmer just looked down the track again.

"But what I don't understand," interrupted PC Cornish, "is why the station master at Aspall didn't see her get on the train with Carr-Pettiford. He never mentioned it to me."

"Oh, that's because she never got on the train at Aspall," said Miss Smy, still smarting. "I learned only yesterday that the station master at Brockford and Wetheringsett had seen her catch the train that morning. But, like our good Inspector here, never thought that a woman might be connected to the murder so didn't think it worthy of mention. As the train pulled into Aspall station that had only Charles Carr-Pettiford waiting on the platform, Elizabeth Bullingham was already on that train."

Looking around, Miss Smy noticed that Mr Manners was no longer there. Unbeknown to them all, he had quietly stolen Cornish's discarded bicycle and was now pedalling furiously down the Eye Road towards the distant offices of the Framlingham Weekly News.

To Winifred Smy, it had been a problem satisfyingly resolved. To Inspector Herbert Tranmer it had been work. To PC Cornish, it had been a local tragedy, one that he would never be able to talk about without uncomprehendingly shaking his head.

But for Nigel Manners, his stick limbs now propelling him at great speed beyond Kenton Corner, it was tomorrow's sensational news.

Lightning Source UK Ltd.
Milton Keynes UK
UKHW010910260822
407817UK00006B/453